Hamlet Hills

The Glade Theatre

Three Witches Wood

Florizel Forest

Kingsbear's House

Helena's Hut

To Malcolm
L.S.

To my bridesmaids, Gracie, Olivia,
Beth and Amelia, who are forever my
cheerleaders, and perform perfect
loop the loops of their own.
I.L.

A storm is brewing deep inside the Glade.
A crew of sailors, shipwrecked and afraid,
Arrive at an enchanted island home
Where wizards lurk and fearsome monsters roam!

FSC
www.fsc.org
MIX
Paper | Supporting
responsible forestry
FSC® C104723

The Forest Stewardship Council® (FSC®)
is a global, not-for-profit organisation dedicated
to the promotion of responsible forest management
worldwide. FSC® defines standards based on agreed
principles for responsible forest stewardship
that are supported by environmental,
social, and economic stakeholders.
To learn more, visit www.fsc.org

LITTLE TIGER
An imprint of Little Tiger Press Limited
www.littletiger.co.uk
1 Coda Studios, 189 Munster Road, London SW6 6AW
Imported into the EEA by Penguin Random House Ireland,
Morrison Chambers, 32 Nassau Street, Dublin D02 YH68
First published in Great Britain 2024
Text copyright © Louie Stowell 2024
Illustrations copyright © Isobel Lundie 2024
A CIP catalogue record for this book
is available from the British Library
All rights reserved • Printed in China
ISBN: 978-1-83891-590-2
CPB/1400/2747/0424
2 4 6 8 10 9 7 5 3 1

The Tantrum

ACT I

LITTLE TIGER
LONDON

Louie Stowell

Isobel Lundie

In a treehouse, in a clearing
in the woods, there lived
a bear named Bill.

Bill lived with his friends,
Sir Bun Bun, Foxy and
Lady Bushytail.

Kitchen

Bedroom

Living Room

Solarium

Hallway

Bathroom

The four friends loved
to put on plays at their
theatre, called
The Glade.

They performed for
all the animals in the forest,
from the poorest mouse to the
mighty Queen Bee herself.

Their newest play was called...

The Tempest

It had...

a storm...

a shipwreck...

Wardrobe

Props

Director

revenge...

spirits...

magic...

monsters...

and a mighty magician called Prospero. (played by Bill, of course.)

rompt

Carpenter

Stage-hand

Set Designer

Today, our hero's feeling very cross.
It's all gone wrong! Bill Bear is at a loss.
But, just as he begins to curb his rage,
Poor Bill falls headfirst off the stage!

ACT II

Bill was having one of those mornings.

THUMP!

First, he fell
out of his bunk.

Then, his honey
had lumps.

YUCK!

"Surely this day will
not get any worse?"
grumbled Bill.

Soon it was time for
Bill and his friends to
practise their play.

Things went
from bad to much,
much worse...

First, Foxy came
on wearing the
wrong costume.

"You're supposed
to be playing a *heroine*,
not a hen!" said Bill.

"Oops!"
said Foxy.

Then, Sir Bun Bun
pulled down the
curtain in the middle
of a scene and sent
Lady Bushytail
flying.

After that, Lady Bushytail said all the wrong lines.

"This is all going wrong!" cried Bill. "You're all ruining my beautiful play!"

"We'll try harder, we promise," said his friends.

Then, Bill practised his final scene as the mighty magician
Prospero. His big speech was going very well!

"Nothing can go
wrong now,"
he thought.

He strode
dramatically
across the stage…

and fell...

right off
the edge!

Our forest friends all flock around the bear,
As Bill howls loud that life is just not fair.
Oh no! Oh cripes! Oh drat! Oh dear!
Will Bill perk up? The audience is here...

ACT III

Bill let out a howl.
"I HATE THIS STAGE! I HATE THIS PLAY!
I WANT YOU ALL TO GO AWAY!" he cried.

"It's going to be okay,"
Sir Bun Bun said.
He tried to help
Bill up.

"I do not want to do the play!"
Bill shook his head. Bill shook his fists.
He cried. He howled. He gnashed
his sharp bear teeth.
"It's ruined now! I cannot
do this play any more."

"But we need
to perform
the play soon,"
said Sir Bun Bun,
looking at the
setting sun.

"Also, Bill," said Lady Bushytail,
"it cannot possibly go any worse
than it did just now. So that
means it will be better!"

Bill sniffed.
He wanted to roar and he wanted to howl. But he wanted to roar and howl a little more quietly.

Now he could hear all
the animals of the forest
chattering and scampering
and fluttering towards the theatre.
They were coming to see the play.
They were coming to see him!

So he got up from
the ground and dusted
off his furry knees.

"The show must go on!" cried Bill.
"We can't keep the audience waiting!"

"Well done, Bill!" the others said.

They were
far too polite
to mention that
it was Bill who
was keeping the
audience waiting.

The play began.

The audience laughed
at the funny bits.

They gasped at the scary storm
and the even scarier shipwreck.

They sighed
at the soppy
bits.

And when Lady Bushytail forgot a line,
she came up with an even better one!

Queen Bee was so
delighted she flew
a loop-the-loop
over the theatre.

At the end of the play,
the audience clapped and cheered.

When everyone had gone home, Bill said,
"That went so well! I have already
forgotten why I was so
cross before."

"Well, we'd better
all go to bed before
you remember!"
said Sir Bun Bun.
"Goodnight, everyone!"

"Goodnight!"
said Bill and
Foxy.

"Goodnight!"
said Lady Bushytail.

Then off they went to bed.

William Shakespeare's Brave New World!

Bill has quite a lot in common with another very famous playwright from long ago: William Shakespeare.

William Shakespeare was born in Stratford-upon-Avon, England, in 1564 and his plays are still popular today with audiences across the world. Shakespeare lived during the reigns of Queen Elizabeth I and King James I and a number of his plays were performed at court, as well as at his Globe Theatre in London.

During a period of twenty or more years, Shakespeare wrote at least 37 plays, as well as a great number of poems called sonnets. A collection of Shakespeare's plays was published seven years after his death in 1623 – this is known as the First Folio.